To the memory of Paul Galdone
—J.C.G.

For Caryl Van Houten, my mother, who read to me
and taught me to dream
—C.E.

Clarion Books
a Houghton Mifflin Company imprint
215 Park Avenue South, New York, NY 10003
Text copyright © 1996 by James Cross Giblin
Illustrations copyright © 1996 by Claire Ewart
Illustrations executed in watercolor and colored pencil
Text is 16/20-point Lucian
Typography by Carol Goldenberg
For information about this and other Houghton Mifflin trade and reference books and
multimedia products, visit The Bookstore at Houghton Mifflin on the World Wide Web at
(http://www.hmco.com/trade).
Printed in the USA.

Library of Congress Cataloging-in-Publication Data
Giblin, James.
The dwarf, the giant, and the unicorn : a tale of King Arthur / retold by James Cross
Giblin ; illustrated by Claire Ewart.
p. cm.
Based on: Le Chevalier du papegau.
Summary: When his ship runs aground on a strange island during a storm, Arthur sets
off on his charger to look for help and meets a dwarf who tells a curious story about his son
and the unicorn who has befriended them both.
ISBN 0-395-60520-2
1. Arthurian romances. [1. Arthur, King. 2. Dwarves—Folklore.
3. Knights and knighthood—Folklore. 4. Folklore—England.] I. Ewart, Claire, ill.
II. Chevalier du papegau. III. Title.
PZ8.1.G3565Dw 1994
843'.2—dc20 92-34031
CIP AC

BVG 10 9 8 7 6 5 4 3 2 1

The Dwarf, the Giant, and the Unicorn

A Tale of King Arthur

Retold by JAMES CROSS GIBLIN

Illustrated by CLAIRE EWART

CLARION BOOKS
New York

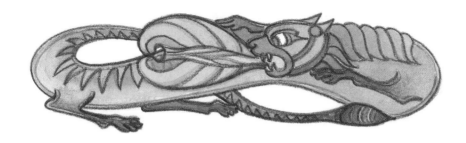

LONG, LONG AGO, when dragons and other strange creatures roamed the world and knights in armor battled them, the king of England died at Camelot. He was succeeded by his son, the brave and handsome Arthur. Soon afterward, Arthur and his company of knights set out on the young king's first sea voyage.

After many adventures, Arthur and his knights were on their way home when their ship sailed into a terrible storm. Bolts of lightning danced around the mast and rain fell so heavily that Arthur and the others could not see even a foot in front of them. They bravely manned the deck but were unable to steer the ship. It rocked back and forth in the waves as if a sea monster were shaking it.

Just when Arthur thought the vessel would surely sink, there was a shuddering crunch and the ship came to rest, its bow tilted upward. The storm died down as quickly as it had sprung up. Soon the first light of dawn showed in the east. Cheered by its rays, Arthur and his men climbed the slanting deck and looked around.

The ship had been hurled onto a beach that stretched as far as the eye could see. Beyond the narrow strip of sand rose a dense forest of tall trees with thick, mossy trunks.

Arthur and his knights dropped down onto the sand and tried to get the ship back into the water. But no matter how hard they pushed and shoved, they could not budge it. At last Arthur stood back and wiped his brow. "There aren't enough of us to move the ship," he said. "We need others to help."

"Where will we find help in this desolate place?" asked one of his knights.

"See that path through the woods?" said Arthur. He pointed to a spot where some of the trees had been cleared. "People may have made it. It might be worth a search to see where it leads."

"Then let us set out at once," said another knight.

"No," said Arthur. "You must stay with the ship and repair any damage the storm has done. I will go on this quest alone."

The knights protested, but Arthur stood firm in his decision. They all ate a breakfast of bread and cheese. Then Arthur had his white charger brought up from its stall in the hold.

After putting on his armor and buckling on his sword, Arthur mounted the horse. He bade his knights farewell and urged the charger forward. In less than a minute horse and rider left the beach behind and entered the shadowy forest.

As Arthur rode along the path, he looked up to see vines with strange purple flowers hanging from the topmost branches of the trees. Harsh cries of animals and birds echoed among the tree trunks. But hard as he looked, Arthur glimpsed none of the creatures that made these sounds.

The path climbed slowly upward from the shore. Off to one side, in the dried mud, Arthur saw what appeared to be a large footprint. It was at least four times as big as any footprint he had ever seen. Arthur thought of stopping to examine it, but spurred his horse on instead.

Ahead there was a break in the trees, and soon Arthur emerged from the forest. He gazed down on the plain below and gasped at what he saw. In the middle of the plain stood a tower. It was roughly constructed of logs and plaster, and rose up, up, up into the air. Arthur was sure it was taller than any castle tower—taller, even, than the tallest tree in the forest behind him.

At the base of the tower was a massive door protected by a huge bar. Near the top was a tall, narrow window. Who could possibly have built such a tower? Arthur felt a twinge of fear and for a moment thought of turning around and going back. But then he remembered how deeply the ship was stuck in the sand. If he didn't succeed in finding help to free it, he and his knights might be stranded in this strange land for weeks or even months. They might never be able to return to Camelot.

Filled with fresh determination, Arthur pressed his legs against the flanks of his horse and rode on toward the mysterious tower.

When he was within shouting distance, Arthur halted his horse, cupped his hands, and called up to the window: "Is anybody there?"

The shutter on the window creaked slowly open and the bald head of an old man appeared. "Another human!" he exclaimed in a shrill voice. "Who are you? And where do you come from?"

Arthur sat tall on his charger, and his armor glinted in the sunlight. "I am Arthur, King of England, Scotland, and Wales," he said proudly.

"England," echoed the man in the tower. "That is my home, but I fear I shall never see it again." He shifted his gaze to Arthur. "What brings you to this island?"

So this place was an island. "My ship was caught in last night's storm and ran aground on the beach," Arthur said. "Now I seek help to free it."

"But there are no other humans on the island except for me and . . ." The old man left the sentence unfinished.

"Then who cleared the path through the woods?" the young king asked. "And who made that footprint I saw beside the path? Do you know?"

"Yes," the old man replied nervously, but he said nothing more.

Arthur studied the man for a moment and then looked up at the sky. The position of the sun indicated it was already well past midday.

Impatient, Arthur turned back to the old man and said, "Since you won't tell me who this mysterious person is, I should return to my ship. My knights are expecting me." He signaled to his horse, and they started up the slope toward the forest.

"No! Don't leave!" the old man called after him. "It isn't safe!"

Arthur swung his horse around.

"Please, sir—stay," the man said. "I'll tell you my story. And then perhaps you'll understand."

"All right, old man," said Arthur. "But be quick about it."

"I'll be quick all right," the man said, "for we don't have much time."

Arthur was puzzled. "Time until what?"

"Don't ask any more questions," the old man said. "Just ride your horse around to the back of the tower. There is another, lower window where I can talk to you more easily. And you won't be visible from the forest path."

Arthur did as he was told. When the old man appeared at the lower window, his chin barely reached above the sill. Arthur realized that he must be a dwarf.

The dwarf gazed across the plain as if he were looking deep into the past, and then he began his tale. "I came to this island much as you did," he said to Arthur. "It happened more than twenty years ago, when my wife and I were servants to the Knight of the Western Isles. We were returning to England when the ship ran into heavy winds.

"My wife was pregnant and due to deliver soon," he said. "The rocking of the ship made her sick. So our master ordered the sailors to drop anchor off this island. For three days we waited while my wife suffered the most awful agonies. And still the baby did not come."

The dwarf covered his eyes with his fists as if what happened next were too painful to remember. Then he went on. "By the fourth day, the sailors had become impatient and, when a fresh wind arose, they persuaded our master to sail on. He took pity on me and my wife and left us a supply of food. But you can't imagine how lonely I felt, sitting with my wife on the beach and watching the ship disappear into the mist."

His voice grew very quiet. "On the fifth day, my wife gave birth to a baby boy. But the labor had taken all her strength, and on the sixth day she died."

17

The dwarf took a deep breath. "Rain began to fall as I was burying her," he said. "I wrapped the baby in a blanket, packed the remaining food, and set off in search of shelter. Just before nightfall, I came to a giant tree with a hollow at its base."

The dwarf paused. "You may not believe what I saw in that hollow. There were three baby unicorns curled up asleep on a bed of leaves like three baby horses."

"Unicorns?" Arthur had heard tales of the rare and wondrous animal, but he had never actually seen one.

"That's what they were—no doubt about it. Each had a small horn growing out of its forehead. As I stood there staring at them, the rain started to fall harder than ever," the dwarf said. "There was only one thing for me to do. Shielding the baby with my body, I ducked into the hollow, being careful not to wake the unicorns. But just as I was about to doze off, the mother unicorn returned to the tree."

The dwarf's eyes grew wide. "She was the size of a full-grown horse with a horn on her forehead as sharp as a spear. And she was pointing it straight at me."

19

"I was so frightened when I saw the unicorn that I jumped up and dropped the baby. I ran out of the hollow and hid behind a tree root."

"You left your own child behind with that horned creature?" Arthur's voice was stern.

"I know it was a terrible thing to do," said the dwarf. "But as things turned out, it was for the best. From where I crouched behind the root, I could see what was going on inside the hollow. My son started to cry, and I saw the mother unicorn approach him.

"I held my breath for fear that she would do him harm, but instead she licked him with her tongue until he stopped

crying. Then she arranged herself so that her babies could nurse at her belly, and my baby son began to nurse with them. After that, they all went to sleep.

"I stayed awake, afraid I might make a sound that would rouse the mother unicorn. The next morning, as soon as she left the hollow to graze, I hurried inside, picked up my son, and was about to rush off with him when the unicorn returned.

"This time she merely looked from me to my son and back again. Perhaps she saw a resemblance between us. Then she nuzzled my shoulder as if to let me know that I was welcome.

"So I moved into the hollow with the mother unicorn, her babies, and my own little son. He thrived on the unicorn's milk, but my food soon ran out. I knew I would starve if I didn't get something to eat."

"Why didn't you go hunting, or search for roots and berries?" asked Arthur.

"I tried, but I was too weak by then—and too frightened of the dark forest." The dwarf stared off into the distance. "I don't know what would have happened to me if a deer hadn't wandered by the hollow one day. He poked his head inside, frightening the baby unicorns and my son.

"I didn't have the strength to deal with him, but the mother unicorn acted at once. Before the deer could make a move toward us, she killed him with a single thrust of her horn."

The dwarf sighed. "That was when I saw my chance. Forgetting my weakness, I skinned the deer and prepared its meat for roasting."

Arthur glanced toward the forest. The sun had disappeared from the sky, and its rays were now slanting through the tops of the trees. "It's getting late," the young king said. "I must return to my ship before nightfall. Perhaps I can come back tomorrow to hear the rest of your story."

"No, no!" said the dwarf. "You must stay to hear the end of the story now." His voice deepened and he stared directly at Arthur. "Tomorrow may be too late."

22

The dwarf's words sent a chill down Arthur's spine. After a last glance at the darkening forest, he decided to heed them. "All right," he said. "Go on with the tale."

The dwarf began where he had left off. "Seeing me eat so greedily, the mother unicorn understood my need for meat. After that, whenever the supply ran low, we went hunting together."

The dwarf smiled as he remembered. "I rode on the unicorn's back, or walked beside her. When we spotted a deer or an antelope or a bear, the unicorn killed it. Then I would tie the carcass to her, and she would haul it back to the hollow. And so the weeks, and then the months, passed.

"The little unicorns grew up and left the hollow. My son grew, too. Before his fifth birthday, he was already six feet

24

tall. By the time he was ten, his height had reached seven feet. He started to go hunting with me and the unicorn, and the more he ate, the taller and bigger he got."

The dwarf chuckled. "We must have made an odd-looking pair. There I was, barely four feet tall, while my son grew to be eight, and then ten, and then twelve feet. . . ."

"How tall is he now?" Arthur asked. He was remembering the giant footprint he'd seen in the forest.

"I honestly don't know," said the dwarf. "If I stood on top of the tallest ladder, I still wouldn't be high enough to measure him."

Arthur shivered in spite of himself. The dwarf's giant son was sure to return home soon. Perhaps, thought Arthur, I should ride back to the ship now, while there's still time. But then he had another idea.

Arthur turned to the dwarf and asked, "Did your son build this tower?"

"Yes," the dwarf said proudly. "He outgrew all the other shelters we built after leaving the hollow."

Arthur gazed up at the tower, which seemed taller than ever in the fading light. "Your son must be very strong," he said.

"He certainly is!"

The young king looked thoughtful. "Then perhaps he can help me get my ship back into the water."

The dwarf's face broke into a broad smile. "Now you understand why I wanted you to hear my story!" he said. "I had the very same idea—that with my son's help we could all leave this place." He paused. "But first we must persuade him not to harm you."

"Why would he do that?" Arthur asked.

A frown replaced the dwarf's smile. "Because he doesn't know his own strength," he said. "I didn't want to tell you before, but six or more men have landed on this island in the last few years. My son has killed them all."

Arthur shuddered inside his armor.

"I'm sure he didn't mean to," the dwarf added quickly. "My son is really a very gentle boy. But those other men foolishly challenged him, and he hit them over the head with his great oak club."

The dwarf went on before Arthur could interrupt. "My son knows nothing of the world. He sees no difference between killing a man who seems threatening and killing a dangerous animal. That's why I didn't want you to leave. I feared what might happen if you met him by chance in the forest."

At that moment, a sound disturbed the quiet evening. It began in the distance, then drew closer until the very earth shook. Clomp! Clomp! CLOMP!

"Is that your son?" asked Arthur.

Before the dwarf could reply, a voice rang out. "Hello-o-o, Father! Look at the great bear I've brought home for our supper!"

"I must go," said the dwarf. "Stay in the shadow on this side of the tower until I tell you to come out," he said to Arthur. "I will go to the other window and call down to my son."

"Father, where are you?" the giant shouted. Arthur could not see him, but he heard each of his words clearly.

"Here, son, here!" the dwarf answered breathlessly.

"I was afraid something was wrong," the giant said. "You're always right there by the upper window when I come home."

"Today is different," the dwarf said. "We have a visitor."

28

"A vis-it-or?" the giant repeated, slowly. "What is that?"

"I will explain. . . ." the dwarf began. But just then Arthur's horse grew impatient at being held in place so long. Before the young king could stop him, the animal neighed loudly and stamped one of his hooves.

"Who is there?" the giant shouted as he stomped around the tower. In one hand he clutched a huge bear. With the other he gripped a mighty club made from the trunk of an oak tree.

Next to the giant, Arthur looked like a small boy. He knew it would be useless to draw his sword against the huge man. But he sat straight on his horse, and his armor reflected the last rays of the evening sun.

"Who are you?" the giant demanded.

"I am Arthur, King of England, Scotland, and Wales," Arthur replied. Looking up at the giant, he did not feel as calm and steady as his words sounded.

"I know nothing of kings," said the giant, "but I can see you are dressed for battle. You must mean to do my little father harm. Well, I won't let you!" He raised his mighty club.

Before he could strike a blow, Arthur's voice rang out. He pointed to the dwarf and said, "Does it look as if I have harmed your father?" Arthur sat even taller and stared at the giant. "No, I have been talking with him as a friend. And I want to be your friend, too."

"The young king speaks the truth!" the dwarf called. "He is a friend, not an enemy!"

The giant looked confused, but he slowly lowered his club.

"That's right, son," said the dwarf. "Put your club away."

Arthur extended a hand to the giant, and after hesitating for a moment the big man reached down and shook it gently. Even so, the shake rattled the young king's armor. Arthur pretended not to notice.

The dwarf smiled. "Good!" he said. "Now we can all talk peacefully." He gestured toward Arthur. "This man comes from our homeland, and he can help us return to it! Won't that be wonderful?"

"Our—homeland?" Again a word seemed to puzzle the giant.

"Yes . . . a place where there are other people like us," his father said.

"Like me?" The giant gave Arthur a questioning look.

"Well, perhaps not exactly like you," the young king said honestly. "But people with the same thoughts and feelings you have."

A gleam came into the giant's eyes. "How soon can we go?"

"We can start as soon as you help the king free his ship," said the dwarf.

"Free it? From what?" asked the giant.

"It ran aground on the shore during the storm last night," Arthur explained. "And no matter how hard we push and shove, my knights and I cannot get it back into the water."

"That will be no problem for me," said the giant. "We'll leave for the ship first thing in the morning. But now it's getting dark, and I'm hungry. We must have supper!"

Arthur tethered his horse to a tree stump while the giant unbarred the door of the tower and put his club inside. Then he picked up the bear. Although the big fellow was smiling now, his size still made Arthur nervous.

But that was nothing compared to what the young king felt when the giant suddenly lifted him with his other hand, armor and all, and carried him up the steps to the top of the tower.

"I gave you a start, didn't I?" the giant said, laughing.

"You certainly did," admitted Arthur as the giant set him down in the middle of the high-ceilinged hall where he and his father lived.

"Don't mind him," said the dwarf. "He enjoys playing a little joke now and then—don't you, son?"

The giant bowed his head shyly. Then he and his father cooked a feast of bear meat in the gigantic fireplace and, after supper, the three of them stretched out to sleep on beds of animal skins.

Arthur had a hard time falling asleep. He turned this way and that on the piled-up skins while the giant's snores thundered in his ears. It wasn't just the snoring that bothered him. He wondered how his knights would react when they saw the giant approaching the ship. Would they raise their swords in alarm and provoke the giant into an attack?

If they did, that would probably put an end to all of Arthur's plans, and neither he nor the others would ever see England again.

The next morning both the giant and the dwarf bustled happily about, getting ready for the trip. Their cheerful mood and the bright sunshine raised Arthur's spirits as he put on his armor.

Suddenly the giant stopped packing the leftover bear meat. "What about the unicorn?" he asked his father. "We must say good-bye to her."

"We'll probably run into her along the path," the dwarf replied. "If not, we'll look for her near the hollow tree."

They all set out for the ship. The dwarf sat in front of Arthur on his horse, and the giant strode along behind. Clomp! Clomp! Clomp!

Soon after they entered the forest, the trio saw the unicorn approaching them. She was on her way to visit the dwarf and the giant as she did every morning. The dwarf introduced Arthur to her, and the unicorn nodded her head as if she knew what the little man was saying.

Arthur stared in amazement at the creature. He had never seen anything like her, and his heart beat more rapidly. The unicorn's white coat looked as smooth as cream, and a long, spiraled horn rose tall and straight from the middle of her forehead. She returned Arthur's gaze with clear brown eyes that seemed to contain a timeless wisdom.

The giant told the unicorn they were going to the ship and invited her to come along with them. She appeared to

understand, for she followed the giant when the little band
moved forward once more.

Glancing back at the marvelous animal, Arthur became
worried again. How would the knights respond to seeing not
just a giant, but a unicorn also?

39

At last the four of them reached the end of the path, emerged from the forest, and began to cross the beach. Ahead of them was the ship, still marooned in the sand.

Just as Arthur had feared, his knights stared in shock when they saw the strange quartet coming toward them. "Is that you, my king?" one of them asked incredulously. Then all of the knights moved their hands to their swords.

Arthur turned to the dwarf, who was still riding in front of him. "Drop down," he commanded, "and try to keep your son calm."

"Who are you, and what are you doing to our king?" a knight called while Arthur was talking to the dwarf.

"Has that giant kidnapped you?" another knight shouted.

Arthur cast a quick look behind him and saw the giant's smile fade. "Those men sound like enemies!" the big man said, and he raised his mighty oaken club. Standing beside him, the unicorn nickered and lowered her head and horn as if preparing to strike.

Arthur's knights moved forward, their swords at the ready. The giant took a step forward also. "No, son, no!" shouted the dwarf, grabbing at the giant's trouser leg.

There was no time to waste. Arthur rode furiously toward the knights, calling, "Stop! Sheathe your swords! This giant is my friend, not my enemy. And he has promised to help us!"

Persuaded by their king's words, the knights put away their swords. Arthur turned in the saddle and saw the giant lower his club. The unicorn raised her head and horn. And the smiling dwarf gave Arthur a smart salute.

Then they all set to work to free the ship. The knights fastened a rope to the ship's mast and another to its stern, and threw the ends of the ropes over the side. The giant tied one of the ropes around his shoulders and the other around his chest, and marched into the water. It only came up to his knees.

The giant gave a mighty heave, and the ship rose up out of the sand with everyone on board—Arthur, his knights, and the dwarf. The giant heaved again, and the ship slid across the beach. He heaved once more, and it splashed into open water. Cheers rang out as the giant untied the ropes and prepared to climb aboard.

Arthur and his men exchanged anxious glances. They feared the ship would sink under the giant's great weight. But after wobbling a bit when he first stepped on deck, the vessel righted itself.

Arthur and the dwarf told the giant he would have to sit quietly in the middle of the deck throughout the voyage. If he moved about, he might rock the ship so violently that it would capsize. "I will stay still, I promise," said the giant.

After he was settled, Arthur and his knights got ready to sail. But then the giant noticed the unicorn standing in the water near shore and gazing up at the ship.

"Look, father," the giant said. "The unicorn wants to come with us."

"Well, why not?" the dwarf replied. "She's part of our family, after all." He turned to Arthur. "May she come, my king?"

Arthur smiled and said, "Of course. We will be proud to have a unicorn in Camelot." All of Arthur's knights nodded in agreement.

So they lowered a gangplank into the water, and the unicorn, her horn gleaming in the sunlight, strode aboard.

When the ship sailed into the harbor at Camelot, everyone in Arthur's court rejoiced to see the young king alive. And after they got over the initial shock, they were glad to see the dwarf, the giant, and the unicorn, too.

To reward his friends, Arthur knighted both the dwarf and the giant, and commanded a gigantic castle to be built for them—a castle as tall as the tower the giant had built for his little father. The two of them, in turn, vowed to serve Arthur faithfully to the end of their days. The dwarf entertained visitors to Arthur's court with his marvelous tales. The giant patrolled the borders of the kingdom with his mighty club, scaring away anyone who tried to invade it.

As for the unicorn, Arthur had a special park created for her in the center of Camelot. In the park stood a great oak tree with a hollow at its base, just like the one in which the unicorn had cared for the giant when he was a baby.

Her friends, the dwarf and the giant, could visit the unicorn every day. Arthur and his knights and the people of Camelot could admire her, too—the only tame unicorn to be seen anywhere in the world.

And thus the dwarf, the giant, and the unicorn lived happily ever after in King Arthur's realm.

Author's Note

This story is the concluding episode in a little-known Arthurian romance titled *Le Chevalier du Papegau* ("The Knight of the Parrot"), which was written in France in manuscript form in the late fifteenth or early sixteenth century, probably in the southern French city of Lyon.

A German version of *Le Chevalier du Papegau* was published in 1896, and the first English translation of the complete work, made by Thomas E. Vesce, appeared in 1986.

Although King Arthur has just begun his reign when the story takes place, *Le Chevalier du Papegau* was one of the last books to be written about him in the Middle Ages. This is also one of the few tales about unicorns in which the marvelous creature is a female. Almost all of the other unicorns one encounters in literature are male.

Le Chevalier du Papegau was written originally for an adult audience. But I felt young readers would appreciate the characters and action in this episode, so I have retold it for them as a story in its own right.

—J.C.G.

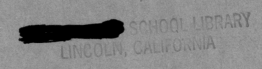